The Farmer in the Dell

Illustrated by
Kathy Parkinson

ALBERT WHITMAN & COMPANY, NILES, ILLINOIS

For Sarah

Illustrations © 1988 by Kathy Parkinson
Published in 1988 by Albert Whitman & Company
Published simultaneously in Canada by General Publishing, Limited, Toronto
10 9 8 7 6 5 4 3 2 1

64646

Library of Congress Cataloging-in-Publication Data

Parkinson, Kathy.
    The farmer in the dell.

    Summary: An illustrated version of the nursery
rhyme is accompanied by music.
    1. Nursery rhymes, American.   2. Children's poetry,
American.   3. Folk-songs, American.   4. Children's
songs, American.   [1. Nursery rhymes.   2. Folk songs,
American.]   I. Title.
PZ8.3.P225Far   1988   398'.8   87-25322
ISBN 0-8075-2271-6

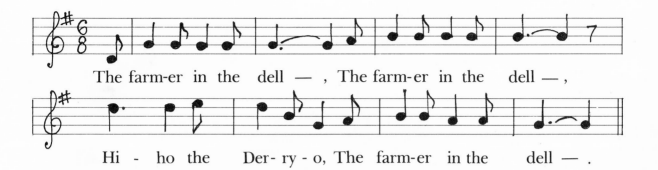

The farm-er in the dell — , The farm-er in the dell — ,

Hi - ho the Der- ry - o, The farm-er in the dell — .

The farmer in the dell,

The farmer in the dell,

Hi-ho the Derry-o,

The farmer in the dell.

The farmer takes a wife,

The farmer takes a wife,

Hi-ho the Derry-o,

The farmer takes a wife.

The wife takes a child,

The wife takes a child,

Hi-ho the Derry-o,

The wife takes a child.

The child takes a nurse,

The child takes a nurse,

Hi-ho the Derry-o,

The child takes a nurse.

The nurse takes a dog,
The nurse takes a dog,

Hi-ho the Derry-o,
The nurse takes a dog.

The dog takes a cat,
The dog takes a cat,

Hi-ho the Derry-o,
The dog takes a cat.

The cat takes a rat,
The cat takes a rat,

Hi-ho the Derry-o,
The cat takes a rat.

The rat takes the cheese,
The rat takes the cheese,

Hi-ho the Derry-o,
The rat takes the cheese.

The cheese stands alone,
The cheese stands alone,
Hi-ho the Derry-o,
The cheese stands alone!